TANGLE AND THE FIRESTICKS

Benedict Blathwayt

WALKER BOOKS
LONDON

First published 1987 by Julia MacRae Books
This edition published 1993 by Walker Books Ltd,
87 Vauxhall Walk, London SE11 5HJ
Copyright © 1987 Benedict Blaythwayt
Printed and bound in Hong Kong by the South China Printing Co. (1988) Ltd
British Library Cataloguing in Publication Data
A catalogue record for this book is available from the British Library.
ISBN 0-7445-3039-3

It was early morning in the Northwoods.
Tangle woke from his dreams of deep
winter snow to find the summer sun
streaming down the burrow ladder.
"I can smell adventure," he said to
himself as he dressed.

The whole forest shone green and inviting.
Although he should have set out for work,
it seemed too good a day for berry-picking
or gathering twigs. Tangle wanted excitement.

He climbed a young birch tree and jumped
from its branches onto the antlers of a
moose.

"Watch out!" he shouted, as the moose thundered through the undergrowth, scattering the little people of the Northwoods.

"You're nothing but a nuisance and a show-off!" they called out after him.

But Tangle wasn't bothered. He swung neatly from the moose's antlers into the trees. "A feather in my cap, that's just what I need," whispered Tangle, as he crawled stealthily towards a still and silent owl. But the owl was not asleep.

"Look what you've done now!" shouted his friends. "You're a lazy good-for-nothing trouble-maker."

Tangle just shrugged his shoulders and ran off deep into the forest to escape their grumbling. Perhaps he went further than he should have done. But the fox cubs were pleased to see him, and glad of a good rough and tumble. Over and over they rolled. It was a great game.

The mother fox, returning to her cubs, barked angrily. Who was this strange furry creature who dared to trespass on her territory? This time Tangle was very frightened. He scrambled from under the cubs and ran for his life. He ran as he had never run before, but the heavy thud of the vixen's paws were always close behind.

The fox followed him all the way home, gaining at every leap and bound.

Tangle knew that if he tripped it would be the end of him.
He was nearly there! He dived headlong into the first burrow
he came to and shut his eyes . . .

. . . Crash! He found himself in a huge
burrow. The Fire Cave! Tangle's heart sank.
Nobody was ever allowed in the Fire Cave
except the Old Ones and the guard.

   Spark, the duty guard, was furious with
Tangle: "Don't you know the rules!" He shook
his fist. "You're in deep trouble this time."
He led Tangle away to the council of the
Old Ones.

Tangle hung his head. He knew how important the Fire Cave was; it housed the First Fire which ancient Northwoodsmen had taken from a lightning-struck tree. The fire had been tended from generation to generation and had never been allowed to go out.

In summer the smaller burrows were hot and needed no fires, but at the beginning of every winter when it grew dark and cold, their fires were lit with burning twigs carried from the First Fire.

If ever there was an accident and the First Fire went out . . .? A winter without fire was unthinkable.

"Tangle, you bring nothing but trouble and danger to us all," said the Chief of the Old Ones. "You must go and live apart from us until you can make up your mind to behave sensibly and do your fair share of work. A time on your own may help you to think clearly."

No-one ever disobeyed the Old Ones.
Tangle was banished to the trees, and
there he stayed, away from his friends
and unable to join in anything at all.
He quickly became bored and unhappy.
"How can I change the way I am?" he said
to himself. "Anything is better than just
sitting here. I shall go far away, beyond
the mountains, and I'll never come back."

Tangle gathered together the things he
imagined he might need on a long journey.
His friends Ember, Star, Ash and Burr,
watched him as he packed.

"Don't go far," said Ash. "No-one has ever
been very far, not even the Old Ones."

"Be careful," whispered Star.

"We'll miss you," sniffed Ember and Burr
together.

Tangle dragged his boat down to the marshy ground. His friends waved goodbye from the edge of the forest.

After one long last look over his shoulder, Tangle slid his boat to the water's edge. He took a deep breath. This was it, he was off!

That first night away from home was not a
happy one. The stones on which he lay were
cold and hard. Tangle felt lonely. He missed
the earthy comfort of his burrow and the
chattering of his friends.

But by morning his troubled dreams had
melted away in the warmth of the sun. This
was a new day and a new world! Tangle set
off again, his heart singing; he felt as if
this was what he had been waiting to do
all his life.

For many days and nights Tangle travelled.
It seemed to him the mountains never drew any
nearer, yet every bend in the river brought
something new and exciting. He learned to fish
and find food for himself; he learned to repair
holes in his boat and to build shelters to
sleep in during the cold nights. He felt as
strong and free as an eagle.

When at last he reached the mountains,
Tangle began to climb. It was hard work, up and
up. He began to think he would never reach the
top and see what lay beyond.

But he did.

Tangle had never seen such tall trees or so wide a
river. He was determined to explore further. What fish
there might be in such a river! The thought made
him hungry. He clambered down the cliffs to the river
bank. There, on the round boulders, he watched and
waited. A huge fish swam close by. Tangle threw
his spear . . .

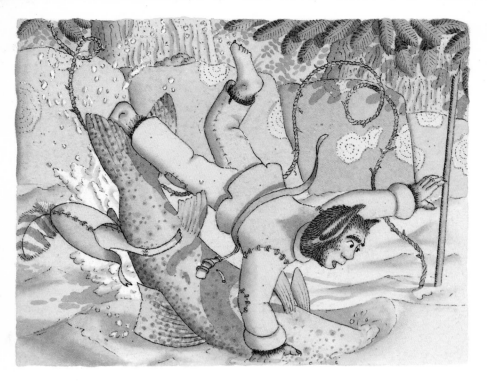

Over and over rolled Tangle, his ears filled with the white roar of falling water, and then down, down . . . This is the end of me, he thought, before the dark silence pressed in on him.

When he woke, Tangle was terrified. A giant hand carried him from the water's edge to a camp among the trees. Tangle felt sure he was going to be cooked for breakfast but the giant dried him in front of a fire and gave him strange and good things to eat.

Tangle quickly realised that the gentle giant meant him no harm. As the days went by they became good friends. They enjoyed being together and Tangle helped the giant in every way he could.

Each evening the giant gathered sticks and logs to build a camp fire. Tangle helped by gathering the small dry twigs they needed to give the fire a good start. He watched closely each time the giant struck one of his firesticks. The giant's fire was a great mystery and wonder to Tangle.

Then came the day when a noisy skein of geese flew low overhead travelling south to lands where the winter would be less cold. Summer was coming to an end; there was the crisp smell of frost in the air. Tangle felt a sudden loneliness and longing for his own people. His friends Ash and Star, Burr and Ember, would they remember him? And had the Old Ones forgiven him yet? He had been away from home a long time and his adventures had taught him many things.

"I have to go home," Tangle explained to the giant, and hoped he would understand. The giant packed a handkerchief with farewell presents for his little friend and seemed sorry to see him go.

"Goodbye," said Tangle, "I shall miss you."

Now the journey back began. Sometimes it was difficult and dangerous.
Each night seemed colder than the last and Tangle felt so very far from home.

An icy wind blew from the North; the first snow began to fall.
Tangle grew weary but day after day he struggled on. Surely he would soon be home.

And then one bitterly cold day he *was* home! He gave a shout of joy when he came through the trees and saw his friends again, but no-one took any notice of him. The Northwoods people were hunched and heavy with despair.

"Whatever is the matter?" asked Tangle. "What has happened?"

"It's the First Fire," said Spark. "There was a violent summer rainstorm and the forest stream burst its banks and flooded the Fire Cave. The First Fire has gone out."

"What shall we do," said Burr, "with no fires to warm us and the worst of the winter still to come?"

"We shall freeze to death," sniffed Ember.

A smile spread across Tangle's face. "Let me tell you of my adventures beyond the mountains. I met a giant, he was ten times as tall as we are . . ."

"Do shut up, Tangle!" snapped Star. "We can do without any of your nonsense now."

"If it's not true," said Tangle, "then where did I get these . . .?" He spread out all the gifts the giant had given him.

"What is this?" asked Spark, picking up one of the giant's presents.

"That's a firestick," said Tangle. "Fetch some dry moss and sticks and I'll show you what it does."

Tangle struck the firestick hard across the side of a rough stone. The firestick spat a shower of sparks and burst into flames. He lit the pile of twigs and dry leaves and very soon there was a bright fire burning. The Northwoods people were amazed and delighted. They grabbed flaming sticks and carried them triumphantly down to their frozen burrows. Soon a fire was roaring in every hearth, and warmth crept slowly back into the chilled bones of the little people.

That night the Old Ones solemnly relit the First Fire. Then a huge feast was prepared in
the Great Burrow and while a blizzard howled through the forest above, the Northwoods people ate
and drank in Tangle's honour. There was much joking and laughter.

Tangle knew for certain that he had been forgiven. He was happy to be home at last.